For my gorgeous children Sam, Ben and Zoe.
And for Rohan. JF

First published in the UK in 2018
by New Frontier Publishing Europe Ltd
93 Harbord Street, London SW6 6PN
www.newfrontierpublishing.co.uk

ISBN: 978-1-912076-50-5 (HB)

A CIP catalogue record for this book is available from
the British Library.

Designed by Celeste Hulme
Printed in China
10 9 8 7 6 5 4 3 2 1

LUCIA
& LAWRENCE

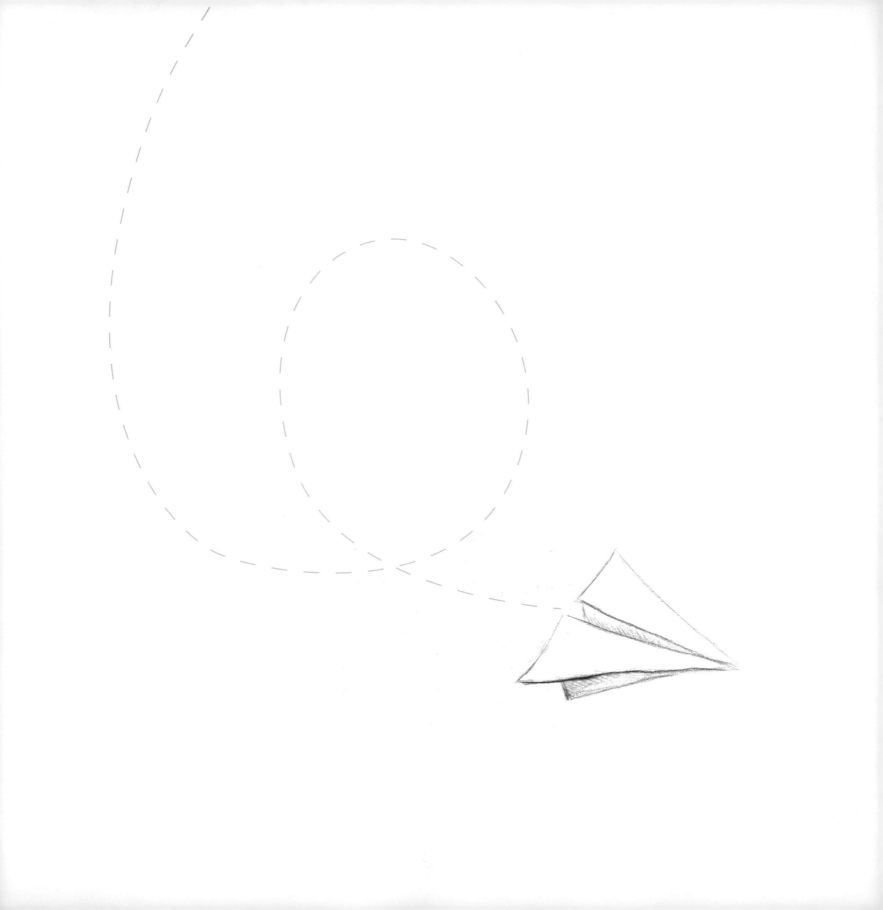

LUCIA
& LAWRENCE

Joanna Francis

Lucia and Lawrence are next-door neighbours.

Lucia has a head full of dreams that reach as high as the sky
and as deep as the sea.

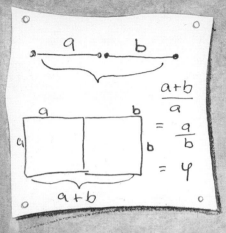

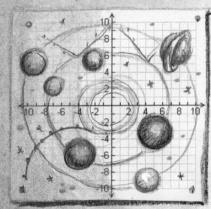

Lawrence has a head full of numbers that are
useful, predictable and safe.

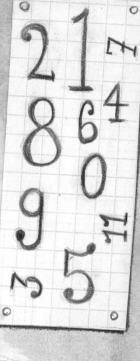

Lucia couldn't remember when Lawrence had moved into the house next door. One rainy day she noticed him.

Of course, the only proper thing to do
was to introduce herself.

It was a rocky start ...

'Lawrence, can you imagine if a rainbow appeared that stretched from my window ...

When the rain finally stopped,
Lucia burst from the house, ready
to cover herself in sunshine.

Lawrence didn't notice the weather ...
but he noticed Lucia!

Lawrence didn't come.

'This is my robot, Fred,' said Lawrence.
'I made him from cardboard boxes.'

'Hi Fred. I'm Lucia.'

Then Lucia shared her world too.

Soon that warm, bubbly friendship feeling wrapped itself around them.

So Lucia asked Lawrence to her birthday party,
And he said ...

'No.'

It was a wonderful party.
All Lucia's friends were there,
except one ...

... who was celebrating Lucia's birthday
in his own way.

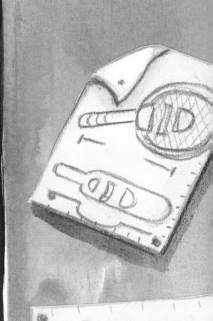

That night a message arrived. 'I hope you had a good birthday. I made you something.'

Lawrence waited all the next day for
Lucia to come. It was a long day.

Then she came ...
bringing that warm, bubbly
friendship feeling with her ...

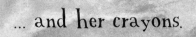

... and her crayons.

Now, when Lucia starts dreaming and Lawrence starts
writing down numbers ...

... they both know something wonderful will happen.